Always Ours

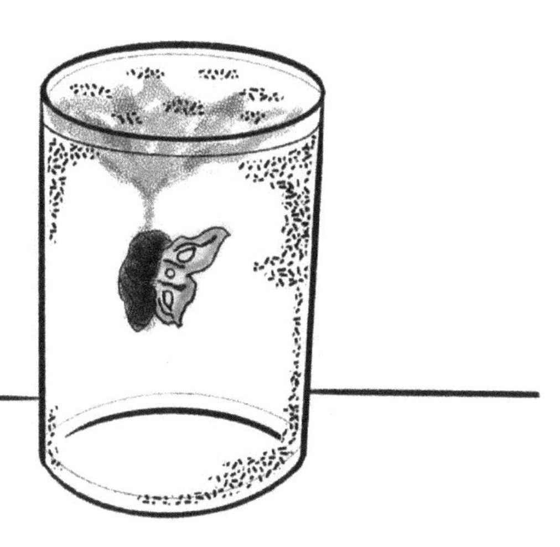

Christy Wopat

Illustrated by Julie Wells

This book is in memory of

____

Published by Orange Hat Publishing 2020
ISBN 978-1-64538-123-5

Always Ours
Written by Christy Wopat
Illustrated by Julie Wells

For information, please contact:

Orange Hat Publishing
www.orangehatpublishing.com
Waukesha, WI

To Aiden + Sophie, who made me a mother, and to Avery + Evan, who help me remember they are always ours.

- C.W.

For George, Therese, and Mary Noelle: our family's little angels.

- J.W.

“Hey, Erin?” Mae whispered. “Do you think anybody is coming in tonight?”

“I don’t know. I don’t think so. I think Mama is already asleep.” Erin’s voice was so low, Mae almost couldn’t hear.

“Ok. Well, I guess we should go to sleep, then,” Mae said.

“Yep. School day tomorrow,” Erin answered. With that, Erin carefully folded back her blanket and padded to the door. She closed it without making so much as a sound, flipped out the lights, and crawled into Mae’s bed. Grasping hands, they began to quietly sing Mama’s lullaby:

“Good night, my love, good night.
I’ll sing you a lullaby.
Sleep, my love, sleep.
It’s time for you to sleep.”

“Love you, Mae.”

“Love you, Erin.”

"Good morning, Papa," Erin called, enveloping her dad with a tight hug around the middle.

"Good morning, girls. Did you have a good night's sleep?" Papa asked.

"Oh, no!" Mae cried out. "I forgot to do my caterpillar homework! Papa, can you help me before you drive us to school? I have to draw a crystal-ness."

Papa and Erin laughed.

"Do you mean a chrysalis?" Erin asked.

"That's what I said. A crystal-ness," Mae repeated.

"I'd love to help, Mae, but Mom and I have an appointment. Sarah's mom, Nancy, will be here soon to take you to school. Can you grab something quick to eat before you have to head out?"

Erin's eyes flashed with disappointment. "I just wish I could ride with you," she whispered.

"I'm sorry, Erin," Dad said. "I really am. We'll get through this, I promise."

What are we getting through? Mae wondered. She followed Erin to the front door to start pulling on their shoes and coats.

"Mae, honey?" Mae's teacher, Ms. Green, said. "Are you alright? It's not like you to spend so much time day-dreaming. You haven't even touched your investigation sheet, and it's for our caterpillars. Your favorite!"

"Wh-what? Oh, yes. Caterpillars. Sorry, Ms. Green. I'm just…worried."

Ms. Green knelt down next to Mae. "I see. Worrying is the worst. But, imagine this: what if a caterpillar fought its way out of the pupa too soon because it was worried about what was happening? Would he ever be able to become a beautiful butterfly?"

"Well…I guess not."

"Right," said Ms. Green. "So sometimes, like caterpillars and butterflies, we need to just kinda hang in there."

"That makes sense," Mae answered, smiling, and then picked up her pencil and got to work.

"Mama? Are you in there?"

Erin pushed the door open just a bit, and saw Mama's eyes glinting in the moonlight.

"I'm awake, Little Goose! Come on in here."

Erin crawled into the giant bed and settled into her favorite place, the crook of her mother's arm.

"Mama?" Erin whispered again, this time directly into her mother's hair, making it blow back a little. "What's the matter?"

Mama gave out a *looooong* sigh, and then smoothed Erin's hair, tucking a strand behind her ear. "Oh, Sweet Pea," she said tenderly. "You're too little to worry about all this. Besides, it's bedtime."

With that, Mama pulled Erin close and began to sing:

"Good night, my love, good night.
I'll sing you a lullaby.
Sleep, my love, sleep.
It's time for you to sleep."

"Love you, Erin."

"Love you, Mama."

"Mae!
Mae!
Wake up!
Wake up
RIGHT
NOW!"

Erin shook Mae as
hard as she could.

“What is it? What’s wrong?” Mae muttered sleepily. “I’m asleep,” she told Erin.

“Mae! It’s Mama. She has to go to the hospital. Our baby brother is coming! Grandma is here to get us!”

Mae bolted out of bed. “James? James is coming? Well, what are we waiting for?” she laughed, jumping off her bed and pulling on her bathrobe.

“You, Mae,” Erin giggled. “We’re waiting for you.”

"Hey, Grammy?" Mae asked.

"Is it time yet?"

“Well, Mae, it’s almost time. We want to make sure Mama and Papa are ready for us.”

“But,” Erin piped in. “Don’t they want us there? James has to be here by now—right?”

“Well, right,” said Grammy. “And of course they want you there. I’ll tell you what—let’s leave now so we can go get some lunch and stop to buy some beautiful flowers for Mama. How does that sound?”

Mae hopped up, sending her popcorn flying. “That sounds magnificent! Here we come, baby brother!”

welcome
baby

It's A BOY!

Finally, the time came for the girls to meet James. Mama looked up at them when they entered, and she smiled even though tears were streaming down her face.

"I'm so glad you're here," Mama said.

"Girls, go sit on the couch, please," Papa said tenderly. "We need to talk about something."

As the girls sat, Papa came over next to them, holding the bundle tightly to him. "Erin, Mae, this is your baby brother James. He was very, very sick when he was in your mom's tummy. After he was born, he didn't get better and his lungs were having trouble with his breathing. He died, my loves, and we are so sad. We are so, so sad."

Mae stared at the bundle of blankets. Nothing made sense. How could a baby be so sick? Can you catch a cold inside a mommy's tummy? And, he was a baby. Babies didn't die, older people did.

Right?

Erin spoke up.

"Mama? Are you sick, too?

Are you going to die, too?" she asked, her eyes as big as the moon.

"No, no, I am not sick. I am ok—please don't be scared about that," Mama said, coming over to sit next to Erin.

"Mama," Erin started again. "Why didn't we die when we were born? Why did James get sick, but not us?"

"We don't know," Papa answered. "We'll never know. But we are so, so glad you didn't. And we hate that this happened." Papa looked down, his eyes heavy with tears.

"Can I see him?" piped up Mae suddenly.

Mama and Papa looked at each other for a long while.

"Please?" added Erin.

Slow as molasses, Papa opened the soft blue swaddle blanket.

"He's so beautiful," whispered Mae.

“Yes,” agreed Erin. “He looks just like Papa! Look at his nose!”

Grandma leaned in and said, “You girls are so brave.”

“No, we’re not,” Mae answered. “James is our family. You don’t have to be brave to love your family!”

Mama and Papa pulled the girls to them in a giant bear hug.

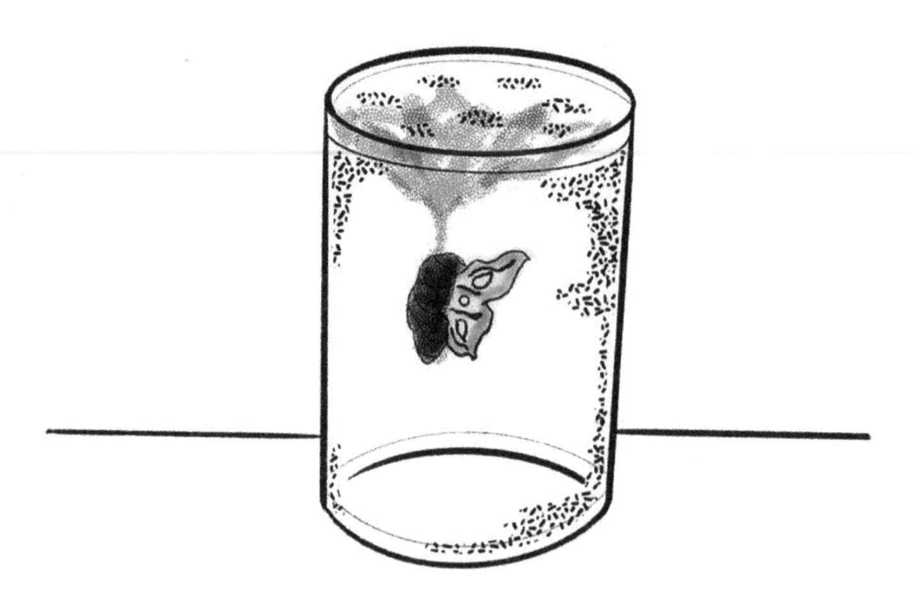

“Ms. Green! Guess what? I can see a wing! Look at how beautiful it is!”

Ms. Green came over. “Oh, look at how strong that butterfly is, Mae! It’s made it through the toughest time of its life, so far, and soon will be stretching its wings.”

Mae watched the butterfly, now almost halfway out of its chrysalis. “Ms. Green,” she started. “Are people as strong as butterflies?”

“Oh, yes, they are,” Mae’s teacher answered. “People are so strong. Sometimes they go through these really awful things, but they find a way to live through them, just like butterflies. People inspire us all the time with their strength, even when they don’t want to.”

“Ms. Green? Do you think you could help me with something?”

"I have an idea..."

"Family meeting! Family meeting!" Erin and Mae called out.

"They're so official," Papa said. "I guess we'd better listen." He and Mama entered the living room to find paper butterflies of every color scattered all around.

"What's all this?" Mama whispered.

"In school," Mae said, "we watched a caterpillar grow and change all the way to this beautiful butterfly. My teacher taught me how butterflies have to be so strong, because they are always changing. We learned that butterflies live their lives not by days, but by moments. And that made me think of my baby brother, James. He is as strong as a butterfly. And he'll always be ours."

Mae then picked up a special paper bag from the floor, motioning for her family to follow her outside. Once outside, Mae reached into the bag and pulled something out.

With that, Mae opened her palm.
The whole family stared in awe
as the butterfly slowly
opened its wings and
stretched them out
toward the

sun.

At bedtime that night,
Mama sang her lullaby:

*"Good night, my love, good night.
I'll sing you a lullaby.
Sleep, my love, sleep.
It's time for you to sleep."*

"Good night, Erin," Mama said.

"And good night, Mae," Papa echoed.

And then, just like every night since he was born, Erin, Mae, Mama, and Papa all said together:

Good night,

James.

CPSIA information can be obtained
at www.ICGtesting.com
Printed in the USA
LVHW022134200520
656046LV00004B/108

9 781645 381235